Born and currently based in London, Paul French lived and worked in Shanghai for many years. After a career as a widely published analyst and commentator on China he is now a full-time author, scriptwriter and historian focusing on China and Asia in the first half of the twentieth century.

His book *Midnight in Peking* was a *New York Times* bestseller, a BBC Radio 4 Book of the Week, a Mystery Writers of America Edgar Award winner for Best Fact Crime and a Crime Writers' Association (UK) Dagger award for non-fiction. His more recent work, *City of Devils: A Shanghai Noir* focuses on the dancehalls, casinos and cabarets of wartime Shanghai. It was a Kirkus Book of the Year 2018. Both *Midnight in Peking* and *City of Devils* have been optioned for television.

French is a regular contributor and book reviewer for various publications including the *South China Morning Post*, *Literary Hub*, CNN, *The Financial Times Weekend*, *Mekong Review* and *Crime Reads*. He also occasionally works in radio drama with productions including *Death at the Airport: The Plot Against Kim Jong-nam* for BBC Radio 4, *Peking Noir* for BBC Radio 3 and has recently completed a 12-part Audible Original series, *Murders of Old China*.

An abridged version of *Strangers on the Praia* produced as a four-part podcast with Hong Kong's RTHK3 was selected as a Finalist for the New York Festivals Radio Awards 2020 – Best Audio-Book, Non-Fiction.

Also by Paul French:

Destination Shanghai: 18 true stories of those who went…

City of Devils: A Shanghai Noir

*Midnight in Peking: How the Murder of a Young Englishwoman
Haunted the Last Days of Old Peking*

The Badlands: Decadent Playground of Old Peking

Bloody Saturday: Shanghai's Darkest Day

Supreme Leader: The Making of Kim Jong-un

*Betrayal in Paris: How the Treaty of Versailles Led to China's
Long Revolution*

The Old Shanghai A-Z

*Through the Looking Glass: China's Foreign Journalists from
Opium Wars to Mao*

*Carl Crow – A Tough Old China Hand: The Life, Times, and
Adventures of an American in Shanghai*

North Korea Paranoid Peninsula – A Modern History

STRANGERS ON THE PRAIA

A TALE OF REFUGEES AND
RESISTANCE IN WARTIME MACAO

Paul French

BLACKSMITH BOOKS

Strangers on the Praia

ISBN 978-988-79638-9-9

Published by Blacksmith Books
Unit 26, 19/F, Block B, Wah Lok Industrial Centre,
37-41 Shan Mei Street, Fo Tan, Hong Kong
Tel: (+852) 2877 7899
www.blacksmithbooks.com

Picture credits
The photographs on pages 35, 36 & 49 were taken by Mel Jacoby in
1937. Courtesy of Bill Lascher.
The 1922 map of Macao on pages 50 & 51 is courtesy of Jonathan
Wattis of Wattis Fine Art, Hong Kong.
The passport image on page 53 is courtesy of Neil Kaplan
of ourpassports.com.
The photograph on page 73 is from A. Bonningue, *La France à
Kouang-Tchéou-Wan*, Éditions Berger-Levrault, 1931.
The map on page 89 is courtesy of the Research Centre Collection
of the Australian War Memorial.
The images on pages 32, 44 & 75 are from the author's collection.
The images on pages 19, 24, 33, 56, 61, 64 & 76 are public domain.

CONTENTS

Introduction – An "Oriental Casablanca" 7

Strangers on the Praia

Chapter 1 – Macao: A route to freedom?. 17

Chapter 2 – On from Shanghai. 31

Chapter 3 – There is no way out of Macao 47

Chapter 4 – Free China. 69

Macao and World War II – A timeline 81

Escape from Macao. 87

Further reading 91

Acknowledgements 95

INTRODUCTION

An "Oriental Casablanca"

At the very start I must admit that *Strangers on the Praia* is an incomplete story. It is, as they say, based on a number of true stories, but history has chosen not to reveal all the details to us. This is as frustrating for the reader as it is for the author. However, the story of those few European Jewish refugees from fascism who arrived in Macao remains worth telling.

It is perhaps a footnote to a footnote in that my research into these refugees came out of a much longer and ongoing research project concerning the approximately 25,000 Jewish refugees who made it to Shanghai during World War II. Perhaps only a couple of hundred of those then found a way, or opted to continue their exodus, onwards to Macao (and perhaps a few more arrived from Hong Kong after the colony's fall on Christmas Day, 1941). It was a tiny percentage of the Shanghai Jews, and yet their motives for moving on, their experiences in Macao,

7

and whether it did prove a route to a better life has long intrigued me.

In part I was curious because Macao itself has long fascinated me. While the bulk of my research and writing has concerned the lives of the foreign communities in Shanghai and Peking between the world wars, as well as occasional side trips to stories from Hong Kong, Macao has always been there, slightly off-stage, but none the less alluring. Lacking the aesthetic bohemianism of Peking, the modernity and vibrancy of Shanghai, or the *entrepôt* dynamism of Hong Kong, Macao sat there in the South China Sea, fanning itself in the heat, accentuating the exotic, a combination of sleepy backwater and nest of criminality. It was also, for a few crucial years, a refuge.

Visiting in 1939, the English poet W.H. Auden wrote in his sonnet 'Macao' (included in his joint book of reportage in China with Christopher Isherwood, *Journey to a War*):

A weed from Catholic Europe, it took root ...
And grew on China imperceptibly ...
Churches beside the brothels testify ...
That faith can pardon natural behaviour.

Macao was a Portuguese colony, leased as a trading post from the Ming Dynasty in 1557 with Lisbon granted perpetual occupation rights in 1887. These were renewed several times, including by the Nationalist (or Nanking) government of Chiang Kai-shek in 1928. After the First Opium War (1839-1842) and the establishment of Hong Kong as a British colony it was true that Macao had gradually become something of a backwater, its key role in the early China trade considerably diminished by Hong Kong's growth. Macao became increasingly associated in the international public's mind with piracy and gambling, an outpost of sin in the South China Sea. Looking through American and European newspapers between the wars for stories featuring Macao yields little more than exotic travel and adventure tales written in rather clichéd prose and almost all noting pirates, opium and fan-tan. Macao became an international trope for tropical lassitude and casual sin.

In 1938 the (then very well known) French writer Maurice Dekobra published *Macao, Enfer du Jeu* (*Macao: Gambling Hell*). The book was pure "dekobrisme", a term used at the time for his style of novels that drew heavily on sensational journalism. The novel was a best-seller. The French film director Jean Delannoy began shooting a movie version of Dekobra's novel in 1939 before the Fall of France but, when Paris was occupied by the Nazis, he had to stop filming. Consequently, two versions of the film exist – the first, pre-war version, starred the Austrian-

Jewish actor Erich von Stroheim. However, he was an outspoken opponent of fascism (as well as being Jewish) and the scenes in which he appeared were redacted during the Occupation. They were then reshot with the actor Pierre Renoir (son of the painter and older brother of the film director, both called Jean) instead of von Stroheim. Parisian starlet of the day Mireille Balin (later discredited for her wartime fraternisation with the Nazis) was the lead actress and Sessue Hayakawa the leading Asian actor who had been born in Japan though worked all over Europe and America, was trapped in France by the Nazi invasion and survived by selling watercolours and joining the French Resistance. The Pierre Renoir version was released in France in 1942 during the Occupation and then, in 1945 with the Nazis gone, the original von Stroheim version was eventually released. While the Macao casinos portrayed in the film had a reasonably authentic feel the entire movie was shot on the French Riviera.

In 1952 a major French movie, *Macao*, directed by Josef von Sternberg and starring Robert Mitchum and Jane Russell, harked back to a similar image of the enclave as louche and corrupt. The representations of the Portuguese territory in both Dekobra's novel and von Sternberg's film were not wholly inaccurate.

Portugal's neutrality in the Second World War meant that Japan did not occupy the territory, though there was always the threat of a military takeover and Japan constantly interfered in Macanese affairs. However, there was a degree of occupation by stealth. By 1943, Japan had forced the installation of a group of government 'advisors' as an alternative to full military occupation. In part the ability of Macao to remain neutral was down to its wartime leadership under the Portuguese naval officer appointed Governor and Commander in Chief of Macao, Gabriel Maurício Teixeira, and the enigmatic Pedro José Lobo, known to everyone simply as Dr. Lobo.

Lobo was in control of the vital Central Bureau of Economic Services that ultimately controlled the territory's supplies of food, medicine and money. Governor Teixeira and Dr. Lobo worked hard to maintain Macao's neutrality and balance the competing demands of Japan and, close by in Hong Kong until the end of 1941, Great Britain. They were proud when newspapers referred to Macao during the war as a 'City of Peace'. Not all of Portugal's overseas empire managed to maintain their neutrality – for instance, Macao's Asian sister colony of Timor was invaded and occupied by Japan in 1942.

Wartime conditions were certainly straitened in Macao. Food was short, inflation rampant and the colony had to deal with over 100,000 Chinese and European refugees. Smuggling and the black market (*mercado negro*) flourished. The situation became even more fraught after the Christmas Day 1941 Fall of Hong Kong. Governor Teixeira and Dr. Lobo found they had to tiptoe very carefully around the Japanese high command in Macao (based largely in the luxury Bela Vista Hotel) and ensure they were not seen to favour the Allied cause over that of the Axis. Accusations of favouritism were commonly proffered by both sides. However, by early 1942, with Hong Kong under complete Japanese occupation, Macao was effectively dependent on official Japanese largesse for most of its external needs – food imports, trade exports, waterborne cargo and passenger craft movements.

Of course Macao could not remain untouched by the conflict raging across Asia, especially after Pearl Harbor in December 1941 and the declaration of war by the United States and Great Britain against Japan. Macao's refugee influx increased just as the Imperial Japanese Navy effectively blockaded the territory and its adjacent sea lanes. A semblance of trade did continue – rice, gold, tungsten, fuels and other commodities useful to the war effort were traded and some businessmen (including Dr. Lobo) profited immensely from the colony's neutrality. We also know that organised crime syndicates – triads – in Macao were engaged in smuggling of all manner of goods and people between Macao, Hainan Island, Guangdong, the French territory of Guangzhouwan and Hong Kong. These smuggler groups appear to have been divided between those who supported regional Free China guerrilla groups and, in some cases, groups who did collaborate with the Japanese.

Macao was also a wartime centre of espionage and intrigue – an 'Oriental Casablanca', as it has been dubbed. Agents of Nationalist Free China, various communist guerrilla forces (the so-called East River and West River Columns operating in Hong Kong and Guangdong province respectively), the Salvation Society of Macao run by Chinese patriots, as well as the British Army Aid Group (BAAG) were all actively involved in smuggling agents, downed airmen and escaped prisoners out of Japanese-occupied territory. Countering these groups were the Japanese military police, the *kempeitai*, as well as members of the *Tokko* (*Tokubetsu Koto Keisatsu*), Japan's counter-espionage force. Additionally, in the name of preserving neutrality, the local Portuguese *Guarda de Polícia*, the small local operation of the *Polícia de Vigilância e Defesa do Estado* (PVDE – Portugal's State Surveillance and Defence Police) and a small force of black soldiers from Portuguese East Africa tried to keep the peace and protect Macao's neutrality.

Talk of espionage and allied partisan operations brings us to the largely forgotten French treaty port and leased territory of Kwangchowan, now Guangzhouwan and the port of Zhanjiang, located at the most southerly point of

Guangdong Province. As with France's other colonial assets in China (notably the French Concession in Shanghai), Kwangchowan declared for the collaborationist Vichy regime of Marshal Philippe Pétain. Vichy recognized the "…privileged status of Japanese interests in the Far East" and, in 1940, the Japanese established a small observation post in Fort Bayard, the main administrative centre, marketplace and port of Kwangchowan. However, from 1941 to February 1943, Vichy officials continued to administer all aspects of Kwangchowan, including customs and immigration. Consequently, an erratic steamer service, mostly operated by French captains, continued to operate between Macao and Fort Bayard. This was made much use of by Nationalist Free China agents and BAAG operatives attempting to smuggle people between Free China and Macao. Throughout the war, clandestine communications between Free China guerillas, Allied agents and Chungking (now Chongqing), China's wartime capital, were maintained in part via Kwangchowan (see appendix – Escape from Macao).

Much of the espionage activity that occurred in Macao and Kwangchowan in World War II is not known – lost or, perhaps, still hidden in labyrinthine archives in London, China, Hong Kong, France, Macao and Lisbon. And this is why *Strangers on the Praia* is ultimately only a partial tale, a frustratingly limited glimpse at the stories, lives and adventures of those Jewish refugees who spent time in Macao. There is still more to be uncovered; but it is hoped that this short story is perhaps a start.

CHAPTER I

MACAO: A ROUTE TO FREEDOM?

It was the names which first intrigued me. Strange… foreign, neither Cantonese nor Portuguese, not what you expect when searching the archives and records of old Macao:

Reuben, Lefko, Ruckenstein, Kohn, Rosenblum…

I had been looking for traces of those suddenly stateless Jews who found themselves cast out of old Europe and left adrift in that great port city by China's Yangtze, Shanghai. Nansen passports in hand, they queued for visa stamps and paid bribes for Letters-of-Transit in their search for routes to freedom. Previously I hadn't thought of them trying for the coastal islands of Macao, but of course they sought out the foreign enclave in the South China Sea – it was, after all, a potential way-station to neutral Portugal. From Macao, so rumour said, boats departed for Lourenço Marques and Lisbon. More rumours told of the possibility of obtaining visas in Macao for Great Britain, America, Australia, Brazil...

And so they crowded aboard tramp steamers or irregularly scheduled ferries – hugging the China Coast down to Canton and Hong Kong, and there joined ferries bound for Macao, jostling for room with the Portuguese and Macanese fleeing the Japanese occupation of the British Crown Colony. The Praia Grande was possibly a quay for freedom; temporary, but maybe possible. Since October 1938 the Reich Ministry of the Interior had invalidated all German and Austrian passports held by Jews. Their statelessness in China was now total. In Shanghai a Portuguese visa that had been a few hundred dollars *cumshaw* to a corrupt official a year before the Japanese invasion of Hong Kong was now treble that, quadruple. Others got "Banana Republic" passports that allowed them to transit to Macao and on to "neutral" Portugal – Dominican, Cuban, Salvadoran or "third destination visas" to places like Curaçao or Surinam... What those refugee stateless Jews paid for those passes and visas is rarely recorded – we can safely assume it amounted to considerable sums in cash, *taels*, jewellery, bullion.

What then of them in Macao? – I search for them in any way I can – long-forgotten consular records, English-

Macao's Praia Grande, 1930s

language directories and Portuguese *directório* found in used book stores, classified advertisements in newspapers as *displaced relative seeks displaced relative*, mouldering hotel *fiches*, discarded immigration cards; shipping records, self-published memoirs, caches of old letters and those major currencies of wartime that don't yellow and fade or crumble to dust but rather stubbornly persist – gossip and rumour.

I see them on the Praia Grande, the Avenida Dom João IV, wandering into Macao's main square, the Largo do Senado, looking for lodgings, flophouse accommodation, cheap pensão, while they join queues at the few open consulates, seeking to attempt the next step. It's a roundabout route of immense proportions. They are dressed like they just stepped off the *Kärntner Straße* in Vienna or the *Kurfürstendamm* in Berlin. Their attire is all wrong; too constricting, far too hot. They're sweating, though it's a Macao winter. They are wearing the clothes they fled Central Europe in. Shanghai is a temperate city, a city of seasons – the winters freezing cold; the summers humid hot; punctuated by cool spring breezes and chill autumn rains. But here, in China's south, it is always humid – their wools, tweeds and thick cottons constantly uncomfortable. The lucky ones are those who've been through a Shanghai summer, for at least many of them have flannels and linens, summer dresses. From Macao they hope to find renewed passage to Lisbon – back to Europe's shores. Maybe a 20,000-mile round trip of uncertainty, fear and desperation.

Word has passed along the refugee grapevine from Berlin's Jewish district to the crowded *shikumen* lanes of Hongkew in north-eastern Shanghai. There are rooms to be had at the Aurora Portuguesa on the Rua do Campo, a Portuguese-run flophouse, but welcoming, and with a popular billiard room that has become an informal clearing house for refugee news. There are few other alternatives. Even for those Jewish refugees with money the dominating Hotel Bela Vista off the Avenida da

República is off-limits, full of Nazi officials and their supporters mingling with their Japanese allies. So too the Riviera Hotel, on the Praia Grande at the junction with Avenida de Almeida Ribeiro, now occupied by wealthy, and snobbish, decamped British residents of Hong Kong who jealously guard the establishment's well-stocked kitchens. There are camps, hastily erected for Chinese and Portuguese refugees from China and Hong Kong by Dr. Lobo, but conditions are reputedly awful. Most will stay at the Aurora Portuguesa, at least until their savings run out.

They speak in languages not commonly heard in Macao – German, Polish, Czech, Yiddish, Wienerisch… after Shanghai they also have the common *lingua franca* of English. They occasionally try Chinese but theirs, hastily learnt, is Hongkew-inflected Shanghainese dialect, and the Macanese bread and fish sellers at the cheap stalls around the Mercado de São Domingos close to the square speak only Cantonese or *patuá* and don't understand them.

Indeed, local Macanese approach them only occasionally. The beggars know they have nothing to spare. The prettiest girls are offered work in the brothels of the Rua de Felicidade, but there is nothing for the men. They are not labourers and, even if they were, many are too old or infirm. There is no work for them in Macao except to join the queues at the consulates and plead their case for exit visas, try their luck for Letters-of-Transit. They are hidebound by their *Mittel Europa* conventions: formal and stiff of dress; correct. They sweat, carrying their suitcases – it is to be decades before someone thinks to add wheels to a suitcase and make life easier for refugees. They are unable to remove their jackets, they cannot loosen their collars – it is simply not in them. It was not done in Wien, Łódź or Köln; they cannot bring themselves to do it here. It would be an admission of sorts that there is no way back, that they are now formally stateless, cast adrift in an unwilling forced exodus, without place. It would be an acceptance that this situation is no longer temporary, that their old lives are finished. They wipe the sweat from their steel-rimmed glasses with the ends of their knitted ties; they stand in line patiently day-after-day.

In the afternoons, when the visa offices and the consulates close, they gravitate towards the Portuguese-run cafés and bakeries around the periphery of the Largo do Senado. Here they can communicate somewhat, they can recognise menu items. They can participate in the main pastime of the refugee – exchanging gossip:

A Swedish-registered cargo ship bound for Lisbon will arrive in a fortnight. There are no berths but they may take on a few younger men as deckhands;

*You can have money wired by telegraphic transfer
to the British Consulate and the English will not
charge a fee to retrieve it in patacas;*

*The Japanese are going to lease Macao from Lisbon
and turn it into an air force base. There will be
work for us all;*

*Dr. Lobo is setting up refugee camps and we will live
in tents there till the end of this war;*

*A Dutch tanker may pass and will take paying
passengers to Surabaya on Java where they say
nobody cares where you are from;*

*A Free French blockade-runner is coming and will
take only those who pay their price... they will
arrive at night, anchor in the Grand Praia Bay and
stay only one hour. By arrangement, the Guarda de
Polícia will look the other way.*

Free French or Netherlands-flagged blockade-runners
out of French Indo-Chinese Haiphong or Dutch Batavia;
Royal Navy ships escaping the Far East and making runs
for safe ports in Aden, Malta or Gibraltar; an American
troop transport passing; a Chinese tramp steamer that

From Macao's old town up to the ruins of St. Paul's

claims it can make Port Moresby or maybe Darwin…
all false hopes. But for these people – Reuben, Lefko,
Ruckenstein, Kohn and Rosenblum – there is little else
but these rumours on offer.

Portuguese from Hong Kong are living in camps in
their own colony. Their status now is worthless. They once
proudly sent back remittances, boasting of prestigious
jobs in British banks and the largest European *hongs*.
Their Portuguese nationality counts as nought while they
cannot find transit to a Portugal many of them have never
known, never set foot in. They are permanent residents
of Macao now. Portuguese in name – Ribeiro, Rodrigo,
Nuñes, Alvaro – but born within sight of the South
China Sea. They were at best weekend visitors only to

Macao's offshore islands of Taipa and Coloane. They lived in Kowloon, North Point, Kennedy Town. None have ever visited Lisbon, Funchal, Porto; the homes of their distant ancestors. Many would not be so welcome anyway – mixed-race Eurasians, the product of Lisbon's colonial mingling. Now they are clustered in Dr. Lobo's camps, hungry, their clothing in shreds, their teeth in poor repair, with numerous health complaints. The Salesian Fathers of Don Bosco help but there is no money, no supplies. Hong Kong may fall, Singapore, the Dutch East Indies, Malaya, the Philippines too… There are no markets, except the *mercado negro*, the black market, where the prices are astronomical. The Portuguese, Eurasian and Chinese refugees fall like flies in the camps – 10,000 will die in the winter of 1942 alone. Cholera, typhoid, malaria, beriberi, tuberculosis, hunger, hopelessness. A mass grave was rumoured to have been dug for them in northern Taipa.

Yet amongst the refugees waiting, listening, around the Largo do Senado are these outsiders: the Cohens, Weinbaums, Montefiores, Schlagmans. What chance for them?

I fixate on one girl, her story briefly glimpsed in faded records. She is only 21 or 22 at the time of this story. I know only a little about her. I know she is German, a Berliner once resident in the Kreuzberg district, who finished her education at a gymnasium. Ship records show that she came to Shanghai after *Kristallnacht* on the *S.S. Conte Verde* of the Italian Lloyd Triestino line in 1938 – a refugee ship from Trieste to Shanghai via Suez, Bombay, Colombo, Singapore and Hong Kong in 24 days. With her family she followed a path that was to become increasingly well worn – from Shanghai's Woosung Docks to the Hongkew District,to crowded tenements on one or other street of Tilanqiao – Wayside or Broadway, Seward Road or Ward Road, Chusan Road or Tong Shan Road. Hongkew Shanghainese and refugees, German and Austrian Jews living together alongside the bombed-out Chinese of Paoshan and Chapei.

She studied English, Spanish and secretarial skills at the Université Aurore in the French Concession. But both her mother and father died in the tuberculosis epidemic of the summer of 1941 that swept the poorer districts of the city. The Jewish Hospital, once the B'nai Brith Polyclinic, converted to a TB hospital on Route Ghisi in the French Concession was full to overflowing. They remained at home, in their cramped Hongkew lodging house, coughing, wheezing, suffering the night sweats and the weight loss till, both paper thin and weak, they inevitably declined, haemorrhaged repeatedly and finally succumbed. Men in masks, from the Committee for the Assistance of European Jewish Refugees, came and took her parents away. They were buried by the *Chevra Kadisha* in the Jewish Cemetery on Baikal Road in Yangtszepoo. Their records remain; their headstones, and the iron gates to the cemetery that were once adorned with the Star of David, are long gone. She was left alone; orphaned in a strange city. America, Britain beckoned as potential places of freedom and a new beginning, but this was 1941. The only way there was via Lisbon; the way to Lisbon was via Macao.

With no family left in Shanghai and nothing back in Berlin to return to, she took a chance on Macao...

Nansen passports – originally stateless persons' internationally recognized travel documents from 1922 to 1938, first issued by the League of Nations to stateless refugees. They were largely worthless but did give some comfort to the stateless. Named after the Norwegian statesman and polar explorer Fridtjof Nansen

Lourenço Marques – now Maputo, the port capital of Mozambique

cumshaw – a bribe or payoff, from a word meaning "grateful thanks" in the Hokkien dialect

pensão – Portuguese-style small family hotel or lodging house

Aurora Portuguesa – situated at No. 45 Rua do Campo. Originally a bar at street level that attracted mostly lowly Portuguese colonial clerks keen on its billiards room. As the number of refugees in the colony swelled, it rented out accommodation on its upper floors as a pensão and became the main lodgings for most of the young Jewish men and women who made it to Macao. Among this group was a young Israel Epstein who had grown up in Tianjin and was later to become one of the best known foreign-born Chinese citizens of non-Chinese origin to become a member of the Communist Party of China

Hotel Bela Vista – originally built in 1870 and named the Bela Vista Hotel in 1936. Now the residence of the Portuguese Consul-General to Macao

Hotel Riviera – originally the Macao Hotel, then the New Macao Hotel, and finally in 1928 renamed the Riviera. The hotel was demolished in 1971

Patuá – Macanese patois which is essentially a Portuguese-based creole language with a substrate from Cantonese, Malay and Sinhala. It was originally spoken by many of the Macanese community but is now close to extinction

Hongkew – now Hongkou

Dr. Lobo – Pedro José Lobo (1892-1965) was born in Timor-Leste of Portuguese nationality. He studied in Macao and remained there, marrying into an old Macanese family of mixed Scottish, Portuguese and Chinese ancestry. During the war he was the director of the Macao Economic Services Bureau responsible for negotiating with the Japanese on matters relating to food supplies, health and disease issues, and the refugee situation.

He was arguably the most powerful man in Macao at the time, up to and including the Portuguese Governor Gabriel Maurício Teixeira

Dutch East Indies – now Indonesia

Batavia – now Jakarta

Woosung, Paoshan, Chapei – now Wusong, Baoshan and Zhabei in northern Shanghai

Université Aurore – the French-run Aurora University on Rue Lafayette (now the Sino-British College on Fuxing Middle Road)

The Jewish Hospital – now part of the Shanghai Yueyang Integrated Traditional Chinese Medicine and Western Medicine Hospital. Route Ghisi is now Yueyang Road

Committee for the Assistance of European Jewish Refugees – established in Shanghai and financed by the wealthy and long established Shanghailander and Hong Kong Jewish family, the Kadoories

Chevra Kadisha – an organization of Jewish men and women who see to it that the bodies of deceased Jews are prepared for burial

Baikal Road in Yangtszepoo – now Huimi Road in Yangpu

CHAPTER 2

ON FROM SHANGHAI

In a Peking Road office festooned with a swastika and a portrait of the Führer, a German consular officer in Shanghai tells her without even looking up at her face.

"This passport now is useless."

He motions to the large Gothic "J" – *Jüdin* – stamped in her passport. The official speaks in a monotone, without any emotion, never making eye contact.

"This passport now is useless. According to the Eleventh Decree of the German Reich Citizenship Law your citizenship, as a Jew outside of the Reich, is now cancelled."

She realises that, as a Jew, she cannot renew her passport at this Nazi-controlled consulate. She leaves, now stateless, an émigré, a refugee.

But perhaps not without luck. She works by day as a typist in the Shanghai office of the Argentine Bank of Commerce in the French Concession. A busy banking hall

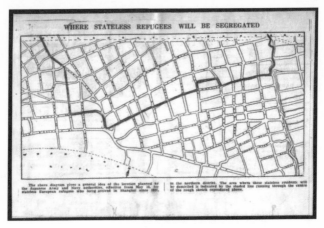

*The outline of the Restricted Sector for Stateless Refugees –
aka The Shanghai Ghetto*

with a polished marble floor, a Sikh guard on the door, a hushed interior contrasting to the noise of Frenchtown outside. There she has met eyes with a customer, a man from Spain who smiled at her. He comes every few days to make a withdrawal and always tips his Panama hat to her. He is so well turned out in crisp linens and polished brogues, with a silver-topped Malacca cane, but is at least fifteen, if not twenty, years older than her. He has substantial funds, yet seems to have no gainful employment. The tellers call him a "playboy", the son of a family who has some relations with Generalissimo Franco and opted to send their son, who is less keen on the Falangists, to Shanghai for his own safety. They raise their eyebrows when they mention that he is a 'confirmed bachelor':

"No interest in ever marrying, that one!"

He is outside the bank one day when she finishes work. He suggests tea; they go to a Russian émigré-run café on the Avenue Joffre, Shanghai's "Little Moscow", and drink tea served from a samovar. He comes straight to the point. He has made enquiries about her and appreciates her situation. The Nazis are pigs, who knows what they will do with the Jews in Hongkew?

The Avenue Joffre, Shanghai Frenchtown

He suggests a marriage of convenience – a *matrimonio por conveniencia*. It is not an uncommon practice in the ever-pragmatic international quarters of Shanghai. To be able to inform his parents he has married would help his situation too. He does not envisage returning to Spain anytime soon; his parents would not be visiting from Madrid. The Spanish Consulate on Bubbling Well Road performs the ceremony for the customary fee. A brief *tetería* in the Spanish Club nearby and a set of wedding photographs at the Apollo Studios on Nanking Road follow, to send to Madrid and assuage the aging parents. And so she obtains a Spanish passport, the passport of a neutral country, and with this, and her new husband's help, she has managed to procure from the Portuguese a Letter-of-Transit to Lisbon and a *laissez-passe* to take a ship to any Portuguese-controlled colony.

A new start. No going back to Berlin; nothing left now in Shanghai. She stands on a back street, illuminated by the phosphorescent glow of streetlights. It is a quiet part of Hongkew. A few Chinese push past, heading home. She is outside a shop with screened windows so nobody can see inside, and with Chinese writing on them she cannot decipher. But above are the three golden balls, the universal symbol of a pawn shop. She is clutching a carpet bag to her chest. She walks to the door, breathes deeply and pushes…

A dark wood interior with a raised counter; counter-to-ceiling bars separating the customer from the pawnbroker, who looks down slightly on the customer. The pawnbroker is an elderly Chinese man in traditional garb, thick spectacles, wispy beard. He does not appear

Wayside Road – the heart of the Shanghai Ghetto

in the least surprised to see a European Jewish woman in his shop. He motions for her to show him the contents of the carpet bag – silver candlesticks, a few nick-nacks, a pewter menorah, and silver photograph frames. He cursorily examines each item and then places them to one side. She reaches into her pocket and passes across some small items: a man's wristwatch, a pair of cufflinks, several rings and thin gold chains.

The pawnbroker works out a sum on an abacus, takes a pencil from behind his ear and writes a figure down on a piece of paper. She frowns, obviously hoping for a little more.

The streets of the Ghetto

"The frames are good silver, and the watch is a fine timepiece too. Swiss. But the gold chains are thin and we buy by the weight in Shanghai, you understand?"

He motions to the items of Judaica.

"These I have too many already. I can only offer pennies. Nobody buys these."

She nods a resigned acceptance, takes the money offered. She turns to leave but the pawnbroker calls her back. He takes the family photos out of the silver frames and hands them to her – her mother and father, outside their Berlin home, the three of them together in the countryside, at the seaside.

*

A Formosan-crewed merchant steamer flying a Japanese flag of convenience takes her three days down the China coast to Macao. The Spanish playboy, her new husband she will never see again, waves her off from the Bund:

"Buena suerte en Macao."

It is a tramp steamer that makes regular trips across the Straits of Formosa and down the Chinese coast. The passengers are mainly Chinese, the only non-Chinese now being Eurasian Macanese or citizens of neutral nations. She is still amazed to consider herself such, with a German first name and a new – and to her, hopelessly exotic – Spanish surname that stumbles on her tongue each time she tries to say it. The journey takes several days and, apart from mealtimes, she spends the majority of the voyage on deck. It is early summer, the weather improving as they sail south towards their destination.

The steamer has iron grilles to protect the companionway of the engines. These are a precaution against pirates. To hear the more regular passengers, many boats sailing close to the Portuguese colony had been seized, the passengers locked in the cabins, the ship looted and then set adrift. The Chinese passengers are mostly labourers who have taken work in Macao but dream dreams of fan-tan and opium. A welcome escape from the more austere cities of Japanese-occupied China. Despite the stories they arrive safely.

Macao finally appears as a blur in the blue haze. Junks, sampans, a Shanghai waterfront of a hundred years ago; Macao a calmer tropical port without gunboats lining the quays they call Praias. Eventually it comes closer and she sees small houses and gardens overlooking a half-moon bay. On a promontory at one end of the town stands a squat lighthouse, perched above a cluster of stucco buildings. Macao's weather is brighter, more tropical, hot and humid. She hears an incomprehensible background noise of Portuguese and Cantonese chatter. It appears to her as she had imagined the Mediterranean, rather than the China Seas.

At the immigration counter she feels a dread as she proffers her passport, a dread that once again, an official will have an objection to her as a Jewish refugee. But the swarthy middle-aged Portuguese official smiles and loudly stamps her passport, passing it back with a half-hearted salute.

On to Customs – a wooden shed, a trestle table, a weakly rotating fan, another swarthy Portuguese official.

"Passaporte, por favor."

Her passport proffered; not a blink from him at the name.

But she sees that the official can tell she is no citizen of Spain. Perhaps he sees this every day, with every arriving steamer. Another Jewish refugee now on an Argentine, or Cuban, Salvadoran or Spanish passport. Clearly no matter to him. He speaks in simple Spanish, the language she should of course speak and which she has, fortunately, acquired a little of at the Université Aurore.

"Cuánto tiempo Macao?"

She cannot however answer him easily, or truthfully, because she does not know the answer, or enough Spanish… so she expresses a wish more than a reality:

"Until the next ship to Lisbon."

He smiles through nicotine-stained teeth…

"Buena suerte, Senora."

Her single suitcase briskly checked, a white "X" chalk mark made to show it has been approved, and she is through, out of the customs shed and in Macao. A new sort of freedom; another temporary haven.

From the Porto Exterior a rickshaw along the Praia Grande, past the grand hotels and headquarters of the Banco Nacional Ultramarino. On through the European and Chinese quarters. She sees many splendid dwellings, fountains, gardens thick with subtropical plants. Further into the old town the rickshaw cuts through narrow, tortuous streets, between low houses, small hotels, gilded theatres and gambling-houses. Chinese labourers hauling wheelbarrows avoid Christian nuns. Such are the contrasts of Macao.

Her destination, as much as she really has one, is the Aurora Portuguesa hotel on the Rua do Campo. The Macanese rickshaw man had assumed she would want that address anyway. The girls who look like her, dress like her, arrive like her, all go there. It is a simple *pensão* in the old town, a converted house with a popular billiards hall on the ground floor, slow-turning ceiling fans, and a small yard at the rear where the young Jewish girls and boys staying at the Aurora Portuguesa gather to smoke and *kibbitz* when the crowded rooms become too hot and airless.

In the lobby a Portuguese receptionist listens to sad *fado* music playing from a wireless. She knows what the new arrival wants. The Aurora Portuguesa now houses only European refugees – all *Judia*. You must pay one-week advance, patacas and give your *passaporte* number for the *policia*… sign here.

Now she shares a room in the Aurora Portuguesa with three other recently arrived Jewish girls, similarly washed up on the tides of history and hatred in Macao. They bunk hostel style – two bunkbeds crammed into each room, lit by a single lightbulb. Her new companions are Polish and Czech. The room doors remain open to allow the air to circulate – washing lines strung across the room drying clothes, stockings hanging, pictures of home – Berlin, Vienna, family photographs. It is a cacophony of the wireless, petty arguments, calls and responses to requests and gossip. They swap well-thumbed novels, old movie magazines, share lipsticks, barter soap.

One of the Polish girls tells her…

"I'm in Macao three weeks now. But no boats to Portugal. No boats anywhere. Only rumour. Maybe Australia, maybe somewhere else. Need English visa for most places. Only English have consulate here that will see us."

The Polish girl touches the thin gold *Magen David*, Star of David, at her neck.

Her roommates spend their time during the day at the Refugee Relief Centre and its canteen, but it's grim, the food is tasteless and sparse, and the room smells of stale sweat. A few of the girls get some work as waitresses; there is taxi dancing if they're pretty.

During the day, between rumours heard in the Aurora Portuguesa's yard, between café stops in the Largo, she goes to the Biblioteca Pública in the huge shimmering white building called the Leal Senado, the building she thinks of as Macao's *Rathaus*. There are some Jews there, other Europeans, Portuguese she assumes, a few westernised Chinese in pongee suits, Catholic Fathers in black robes. Librarians push trolleys of books around, shelving them. She looks at a globe that stands on a sunlit window ledge. She finds Berlin, moves her fingertip slightly to the port of Trieste; a half-turn of the globe finds the China coast and Shanghai. Back slightly and down, her finger traces the coastline – Ningpo, Amoy, Canton, Hong Kong and across to Macao. She hadn't even heard of the islands three months ago; hadn't known they were Portuguese, neutral, miraculous potential stepping stones in the China Seas to somewhere safe. She spins from Macao, almost three quarters of a full turn to Lisbon. Above is Great Britain and then across the wide Atlantic Ocean, over the Azores, to New York. Such a long journey for a young woman; so much of it still to undertake.

When the library closes she walks through the streets of the old town. Past cafés, mah-jong parlours, beauticians, bakeries, food stalls, medicine shops, pawn shops. The panoply of Macao street life. She likes the Portuguese cafés, their interiors – with some Chinese touches – transplanted to Macao. The blue-and-white Azulejo tiling, photographs of famous Basque Jai-alai players and posters for the Jai-alai events at the Macao fronton cover the walls. These places feel European to her, but not the threatening Germanic world she has left, but a new, warmer, Europe she may one day reach.

On Friday evenings she lingers later in the library, reading. As a refugee she can read books, but does not have borrowing privileges. A few older Jewish men, European Ashkenazy and the darker Arab-looking Sephardics, meet in the reference room for the *Shabbos*. Macao has no synagogue and these are pious men, believers. They wish to gather, to mutually support, to pray and, of course, to kvetch. If there is no temple then a house of books seems to them the most appropriate place to congregate.

She waits till they finish their prayers and mingles with them. They wander out of the library just before it closes. They live in the overcrowded *pensão* around the main square of the Largo, on the side streets of the Rua do Campo and the Rua da Barca da Lenha in crowded garrets above the shops, paying by the day. They prefer to find a Macanese *cha chaan teng* café-restaurant that will let them sit late into the evening, lingering over one cup of wartime ersatz coffee, forgoing the non-existent sugar, perhaps slurping some noodle soup for sustenance, an egg tart maybe.

Food is in short supply; coffee non-existent. They say the Portuguese refugees in Dr. Lobo's government camps are starving, wracked with disease, but these men, these refugees, still have a few patacas to spare. They are happy that she joins them. They have daughters, granddaughters, nieces they miss and have no news of, whether they are now in Hongkew or still back in the old cities of Europe. They write letters and post them at the imposing grey Central Post Office on Largo do Senado. They apply the stamps with their saliva – a row of stamps showing Vasco da Gama's *São Gabriel*, his armada's flagship, across the right-hand corner of the envelope. They post them – to Shanghai, in hope, telling their families to follow, if they've arrived. They can never be sure they are actually

sent anywhere; no replies ever come. They are left with little but more gossip:

The Japanese Imperial Army will take Macao next week and put us in a ghetto;

The Nazis at the Bela Vista are just waiting for the Japanese to allow them to take us away;

But the Japanese need farmers in Manchukuo and will offer us land in return for our labour;

Curaçao and Surinam will take Jews, Dutch ships go there, but it is so far…;

A Red Cross evacuation ship may be allowed to dock at the Baia de Praia Grande and take some refugees to Australia, if they have a British visa;

Another ship may take people to Lourenço Marques...
but where is that?

She has heard that rumour before and looked it up on the globe in the Biblioteca Pública. Lourenço Marques is in Portuguese East Africa. The old men say that there is a chance you can get from there to South Africa, British territory where Jews are allowed to live. South Africa might work. If the ship comes, she will try to get aboard.

But what you need if you hope to board a ship in Africa for England, or to enter South Africa, or Australia, is a British entry visa, and only a British embassy or consulate can issue that. It is a faint hope, but a hope nonetheless. She must persuade the British...

Peking Road – now Beijing Road

Avenue Joffre – now Huai Hai Middle Road and once also known as "Little Russia" or "Little Moscow" for the number of Russian émigré-run establishments and shops

Spanish Consulate and Spanish Club – the two venues were adjacent to each other at 1205 Bubbling Well Road (now Nanjing Road West)

tetería – a traditional style of Moorish tearoom found ostensibly in Granada that was recreated in Shanghai's Spanish Club

Straits of Formosa – now the Taiwan Straits

Ningpo, Amoy, Canton – now Ningbo, Xiamen and Guangzhou

cha chaan teng – literally 'tea restaurant' in Cantonese

Manchukuo – the name given to Manchuria after the Japanese occupation of 1932

CHAPTER 3

There is no way out of Macao

By now it is late in the year, winter back in Europe, icy cold (she remembers) in Berlin in December. But to her in Macao the nights still feel humid as she contemplates another day of queuing at the British Consulate in the faint hope of a transit visa. Escaping the claustrophobic confines of the Aurora Portuguesa she returns to the Leal Senado, busy with families, traffic, brightly lit shop windows, decorations, "*Feliz Natal*" strung across the square. She had forgotten it was Christmas. Crowds outside the Our Lady of Penha church atop the hill overlooking the old town. Couples strolling, customers coming in and out of shops, cafés and restaurants. There is little to buy, the coffee is weak, few have money to spare, but spirits seem to be maintained, at least in this part of the old town at this special time of year for Macao's Portuguese.

Returning to the Aurora Portuguesa she senses excitement, and fear. She hears the chatter and realises that Hong Kong has fallen; the British colony so many in the queue believed a bastion of hope has failed them. Pictures of the Rising Sun flag over the colony on the front page of *A Voz de Macao*. This is a disaster; the war has come closer to Macao. The rumour mill says Governor Teixiera and Dr. Lobo are nervous Japan will simply take Macao. To ensure Macao knows how close the Japanese are, their Mitsubishi bombers fly low over the old town from their captured landing strip at Kai Tak in Kowloon. The queues at the British Consulate just get longer.

As a refugee you do not need an exit visa to leave Macao. Macao does not care if you leave, or where you go. You are simply one less mouth to feed; one less refugee taking up space in an already overcrowded Portuguese colony. What you do need is a transit visa or an entry visa... for somewhere. Anywhere. Portugal doesn't care. You can go to the Philippines or Manchukuo, America or England – it doesn't matter to the Macao authorities. That is the beauty of neutrality – you take no side, you show no obvious sympathy, you are dispassionate.

The refugee's problem is that no ship will let you board, nor border post allow you to cross, unless you can show an official transit or entry visa for a destination. Without that visa you become the captain of the ship's problem, or

The view across the Praia Grande from the Bela Vista Hotel, 1930s

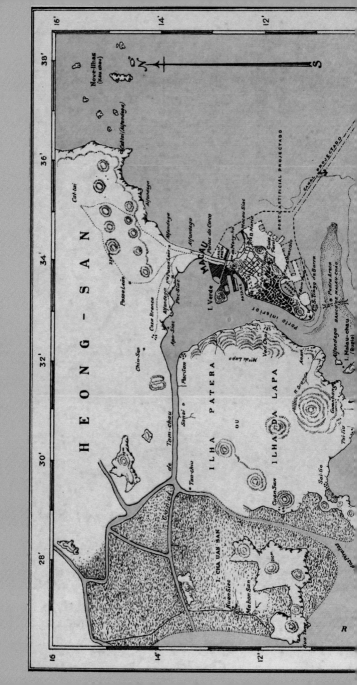

PLAN OF MACAU AND NEIGHBOURING TERRITORIES 1922

A German passport stamped with a "J", 1938

the border guard's headache. She needs a visa; the refugee grapevine on the Rua do Campo says she needs a British visa and so she queues.

With the fall of Hong Kong, Singapore and Malaya to the Japanese there is now no British diplomatic representation left between Port Moresby and India, except here in Macao. Only a lone Union Jack flies, a sole British Consul resides, across more than five thousand miles. And it is on the Praia Grande.

And so she goes each day to the British Consulate. She has little choice. There is no American representation here. Only the British. From the Aurora Portuguesa to the British Consulate's immigration office on the Praia Grande – ominously, perhaps, next door to the Japanese Consulate – is only a short walk, but the weather is humid. She is made to wait daily, with others: Portuguese who once worked for British *hongs*, Jews in hope, once-wealthy Shanghainese who graduated from Cambridge or Oxford, Eurasians who clutch papers hoping to prove a British father or mother, stateless White Russian émigrés with Nansen passes hoping for British passports. The British have placed extra guards on their Consulate door since Hong Kong fell. Most days the queue barely moves. She waits all day and then returns to the click-clack of the billiards on the ground floor of the Aurora Portuguesa.

Eventually, she does see the Consul. She'd thought it would never happen, but her Spanish passport, a passport for a country she has never seen, allows her to at least move ahead in the queue over the entirely stateless.

She is ushered into a grand reception room that has been converted into an office full of dark wood desks with busy typists, clerks in suits, some interviewing refugees. A well dressed, seemingly efficient Eurasian secretary sits at a desk positioned just outside the door to a private office marked "CONSUL". She sits on a wooden bench outside the Consul's office, clutching her portfolio of official papers. The bench is hard, but it is a relief to be in a safe place.

She is ushered into the Consul's office by the secretary. He sits low, dwarfed by the immense wooden desk. He introduces himself – John Reeves. She immediately likes him. His skin looks badly burnt by the sun, his neck is red-raw around his collar and looks sore; he wears wire-rimmed glasses, has thick lips, large teeth and a schoolboy's smile. He is what she imagines a kind English schoolteacher would look like, not a Consul.

The secretary précises her life to Reeves…

"Born in Berlin, Germany. Recently of Shanghai. Jewish. Valid and current Spanish Passport issued in Shanghai. German Birth Certificate. Parents Deceased,

No Dependents. Request for Transit Visa to Great Britain."

The secretary closes her manila folder, places it on Reeves's desk and leaves. Reeves pays no attention to the folder.

He motions to her to pour some iced water from a glass jug on his desk. She does so gladly, being parched. He appears kindly, but his message is firm and clear:

"There is no way out of Macao."

*

At night now, Largo do Senado is deserted. People stay indoors, a Black Out is enforced, people are encouraged to go home by the *Polícia de Macau*. The residents of the Aurora Portuguesa are increasingly desperate. Many restaurants and dancehalls have closed. Work is impossible to find. The food at the Refugee Reception Centre gets worse daily. Even the Biblioteca Pública is only open a couple of hours a day.

Each day she returns to the Consulate. The Union Jack flies limply in a lacklustre breeze. Jewish refugees, Eurasians, some Chinese. The queue snakes along the pavement with uniformed Portuguese police keeping order. Everyone clutches bundles of paperwork in portfolios. There are bored children, couples squabbling, older people sitting on stools. The mood is one of weary

Macao's harbour, 1930s

resolution. Behind them is the beautiful Baia de Praia
Grande with numerous junks and ferries. Just along
the street from them they can see a similar house with
no queue, but armed soldiers on guard outside and the
Rising Sun flag – the Japanese Consulate.

Perhaps there is no way now, but when a way comes
she will need this British visa. She stands in the queue,
in the winter humidity that chills the locals but is still so
warm to these Europeans. They sweat amid the swirling
gossip of the expectant refugees that is as predictable as
mosquitoes and heat rash:

The American Navy will come. They have already taken the Azores from Portugal and will now take Goa and Macao;

Smugglers can take you to Formosa where there are jungles you can hide in till the war is over;

An Italian tramp steamer will moor for one night at the Bacia Norte do Patane and take aboard people for Portuguese Timor, if they can pay. But it is hot and full of cannibals and head-hunters there;

The Communists can smuggle people across to Kwangtung and then into Free China;

Perhaps from there you can get to French Indo-China or British Burma and then…

There is a train south from Yunnan-Fu or a road that runs into the jungle all the way to Rangoon, so they say.

From there… to where? She looks at the globe – Hanoi, Rangoon, Mandalay, Chungking, Huế, Yunnan-Fu, Goa – all mentioned in rumours, but all so far away. She cannot even find Timor. Eventually the kind British

Consul, John Reeves, relents and issues her an entry visa for Great Britain, Her Dominions and Territories, but tells her:

"I can give this to you but it is useless. There is simply no way there from here."

She smiles, not quite following.

"It's too far, there are too many Japanese submarines, there are no more ships making the voyage to Europe now. Suez, the Mediterranean… too dangerous."

She looks forlorn.

"Maybe," he says, "maybe sometime a ship will come en route to Batavia or Timor. Take that ship and then try for Australia. The stamp is good for Down Under."

She doesn't know what this means. "Down Under"?

The dictionary in the Biblioteca Pública does not explain; the old men who gather there don't know either. She has nothing but a useless entry visa for a country six thousand miles away, a dwindling amount of patacas, a few Chinese dollars, and enough credit to stay perhaps another fortnight at the Aurora Portuguesa. Then? Even out in the yard of the Aurora Portuguesa at night, looking up at the stars, sharing a Japanese Golden Bat cigarette with one of the Polish girls, it is too hot to think… she only hears Reeves over and over again…

"There is no way out of Macao."

She takes to siting in the stalls at the Teatro Apollo on Leal Senado. The films mean little to her, but the newsreels, though in Portuguese, show what is happening nearby in occupied Hong Kong. Each day is worse – Japanese soldiers entering Manila; Americans retreating through jungle; short Japanese men landing on Borneo, the disaster of Singapore, ships on fire. Even after Hong Kong somehow she had thought Singapore impregnable. She stays in the stalls, glued to the screen, even as air raid sirens occasionally sound outside.

And still the echo of Reeves's mantra.

"There is no way out of Macao."

She begins to resign herself to Macao; to accept it. She prepares herself, patacas daily dwindling, to accept Dr. Lobo's refugee camp. There is no way out.

But then it seems that there just might be. John Reeves sends a note to her at the Aurora Portuguesa. It is an extraordinary and unexpected request. Would she consider accompanying a Spanish man to the French-controlled port of Kwangchowan? From there, they may be able to enter Free China. Would she be so good as to call upon him at the Consulate at the soonest available opportunity?

She agrees to hear more. She returns to the Praia Grande Consulate. She shows the note to the guard on the door, Reeves's elaborate signature at the bottom, the British crown embossed at the top. It is like a magic charm. She skips the queue and is ushered inside politely. Reeves's secretary greets her and immediately escorts her to Reeves's office. He is waiting and indicates she should sit.

The Secretary returns with a tea tray. Reeves gestures that she should place it on the table and leave. He pours tea for them both. He indicates the lemon slices on a small plate and the sugar bowl. She nods to both.

"*Zitronentee* of course – a Berliner indeed. I assume you have no plans to return to that city?"

He pours himself a black tea, adds sugar.

"I would prefer milk obviously – the English way. But milk, even the awful tinned stuff, is a scarce commodity in Macao these days, even for a British Consul. Reserved for babies and the elderly. One privilege of my position is that Dr. Lobo allows us an allowance of sugar."

They both sip their tea. Reeves examines her over his wire-rimmed glasses, his neck rash looking especially raw. He is honest with her – this man that he mentioned in his letter, he is not from Spain. He smiles. She has known that he had guessed immediately that Spain was as familiar to her as any faraway fairy-tale land she had ever read about.

The man is English, but he must leave Macao as he is wanted by the Japanese in Hong Kong and they will

The Landing Stage, Macao

come here too looking for him. It is only a matter of time. Reeves does not say as much, but she has heard the rumours of the few determined British who have managed to escape from the Stanley Internment Camp and make their way to Macao by boat in the hope of getting back to Britain somehow, back to the war. Men and women of some importance, connected to secret work, with important knowledge to share… knowledge that could change things.

This man has arrived in Macao by sampan. He can speak some Spanish. And so, it had been thought, after some discussion, and careful consideration, that perhaps these two people, both so desirous of leaving Macao, might be mutually beneficial to each other at this time… if the lady was in agreement with the plan?

The territory of Kwangchowan, with a port and small town called Fort Bayard. A forgotten backwater of France's Far Eastern possessions. On the border of China and French Indo-China. A ferry ride of a day or so around Hainan Island. There's a lot of trade between Fort Bayard and Macao. Smuggling, the black market. Everything from cigarettes to vegetables, but the Portuguese don't much mind as it helps the situation here, which would be much worse without the *mercado negro*. The French turn a blind eye too. Others have used the route – neutrals, anti-Nazi Germans, Filipinos moving on. It has worked.

She knows. Kwangchowan was one place she did manage to find in the atlases at the Biblioteca Pública. Essentially a bay along the coast of Kwangtung offering some protection from typhoons, a small enclave centred around the port town of Fort Bayard and demanded by the French from a weakened and bullied Qing-dynasty China in some ancient treaty. Now a sleepy backwater of the French Indo-Chinese Empire, equally forgotten by Tokyo and Paris, it seems.

Reeves can provide the man with a falsified Immigration Office Permit stating that he was born in Madrid. Should anyone ask, he is of dual nationality with a Spanish father and an English mother, though he has, in the turmoil of the last few years, managed to lose his passport and is unable to get a new one due to a lack of Spanish consular representation in the Far East. A simple mistake. However, his wife has her Spanish passport… and so on…

Reeves looks up from his teacup.

"Do you speak French by any chance?"

She has a little French. A proficiency certificate from her gymnasium in Berlin. A trip once, with her father, to Bordeaux where he had some business or other.

It may work, if he is accompanied by a Spanish passport holder and the French are not looking too closely at documents in Kwangchowan. Reeves will supply the necessary vaccination and inoculation certificates required for entering French territory. He has concocted a cover story of sorts. They are a couple heading to Haiphong to take one of the steamers to Sumatra and a job in the Dutch East Indies oil industry. Haiphong and Surabaya are both protected by the Japanese; the Javanese port is Tokyo's major oil source now. They've commandeered the Dutch steamers that used to ply the routes between French Indo-China and Batavia, so it's a well-known service. Reeves knows there are some European technicians – Germans, Italians and Spanish, as well as Dutch – working in the oil fields. They'll doctor some paperwork, letters of employment, qualifications, references, that will pass

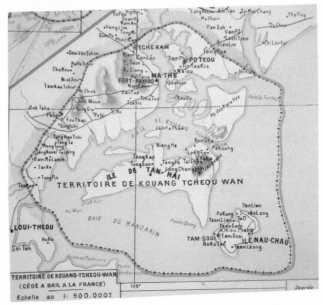

A map of the Kwangchowan French enclave, 1909

muster at Fort Bayard if necessary. There's only a small detachment of French colonial soldiers in Fort Bayard watching for smugglers. Customs, immigration, the police are all still under French civilian administration.

Reeves believes it can work. A married couple will attract less attention; a wife to vouch for her husband. A man and wife from a neutral country of no consequence in this Oriental war. The French post in Kwangchowan is technically under the control of the collaborationist Vichy regime, and if you can arrive on a Portuguese-flagged boat and convince them you are Spanish and moving on out of their territory and responsibility, they may not care enough to stop you.

It is not without risk, but what other hope is there? She knows in her heart of hearts that all the rumour and gossip of the Largo do Senado cafés and of the Rua do Campo is worthless – there will be no blockade runners to Australia, no tramp steamers to Timor, the American Navy is not on the horizon. This is her only chance.

She agrees. Reeves nods and offers more *Zitronentee*.

A Voz de Macao – a Portuguese-language daily newspaper in Macao

Kwangtung – now Guangdong

Yunnan-Fu – now Kunming

Chungking – now Chongqing and then the Nationalist capital of Free China

Reeves – John Pownall Reeves (1909-1978) was British Consul in Macao from 1941 to 1946. He read modern languages at Cambridge before joining the British foreign service. He spent two years in Peking studying Chinese and then served in Hankou, Mukden (Shenyang) and Macao. After the war he was posted first to Rome and then to Surabaya in Indonesia. Leaving the consular service he moved to South Africa and worked as a broadcaster on South African radio

Kwangchowan – Guangzhouwan, with Fort Bayard now the port of Zhanjiang, in Guangdong Province. A small enclave on the southern coast of China ceded by the Qing Dynasty to France as a leased territory and administered as an outlier of French Indo-China until it was eventually taken over entirely by Japan in February 1943. The central administrative area of the territory, Fort Bayard, had a population of, at most, twelve thousand

Sumatra oil fields – with only limited resources of fuel Japan moved quickly to capture the extensive Sumatran oil fields in the Dutch East Indies. At the time the annual output of Sumatra was 65 million barrels annually, which was more than enough to make Japan self-sufficient in the naval war in the Pacific. Some Europeans did indeed work in the Sumatran refineries during the war

CHAPTER 4

FREE CHINA

The date is set. John Reeves sends word to her at the *pensão*. They will depart in two nights' time. He tells her the details of the rendezvous and includes some patacas. She is to use them to settle her bill at the Aurora Portuguesa. She may take only one suitcase, no more; they must travel as lightly as possible. This is easy for her as she has little more than a couple of summer dresses, a cardigan, some underwear and a raincoat to her name now. She donated all her winter clothing to the Emigranten Thrift Shop in Shanghai before she sailed to Macao.

Reeves insists she tell no one of her plans.

If anyone asks, tell them you have met an old friend from Shanghai living on the other side of Macao, in Coloane, and you are moving to live with them, as a governess, a maid, anything you like.

He includes a cheap brass wedding ring with a separate note:

I observed that you were not wearing one when last we met. Perhaps it would be best to have one.

She checks out of the Aurora Portuguesa. The receptionist asks no questions; the Polish and Czech girls in her dorm believe the story about going to Coloane to work. They wish her well.

*

The new companions meet after nightfall on the balcony of a gambling house near the bay, an exclusive establishment patronised largely by middle-class Chinese in white linens who crowd around large gaming tables on the lower floor, chain-smoking and talking rapidly in Cantonese. Mostly Chinese and Eurasian businessmen of some obvious wealth populate the upper floor, some standing by the rail, lowering their bets to the table below by means of a basket, and others lounging upon divans, drinking tea or more smoking. In this time of general poverty she correctly takes them for men of the *mercado negro*, meaning that this gaming house must surely be sanctioned by the Portuguese and so therefore free of raids and a safe place to meet. The Englishman is drinking a whisky-soda, hiding in plain sight amid the glazed-paper lanterns and the layers of thick aqueous blue smoke. He nods to her and she joins him. Nobody pays them any attention. She drinks a small glass of fortified wine for her nerves.

Close to midnight they walk together to the Macao Ferry Terminal, a single suitcase each as instructed. The departures board details the midnight ferry to Fort Bayard via Hainan Island. The only lights are the immigration and customs shed. There is a light rain and she is glad of her raincoat. Inside there is a Portuguese official on duty and a small line of mostly Chinese passengers having their documents checked and their bags searched.

He moves to the desk and proffers the forged documents to the immigration officer, who takes no time to glance at them, return them and wave him through. The official then examines her passport. As ever with border officials her stomach is a mass of butterflies and she always expects the worst. She can see from his expression that he can tell she is not Spanish. But the man only looks quizzical rather than suspicious. Perhaps he is used to Jewish refugees from Shanghai on all manner of passports? He stamps her passport with a flourish and beckons forward the next waiting passenger. The customs officer is similarly cursory, barely makes eye contact and swiftly marks her case with the chalk "X". Beyond, the man is waiting, smoking, appearing casual.

71

They board a Portuguese-flagged tramp steamer, the *King Yan*, heading for Kwangchowan under its French captain on a semi-regular run. She thinks that John Reeves probably bribed the Portuguese customs officials to pay little attention to those boarding tonight. It all seemed too easy.

The Macao-Fort Bayard ferry slips its mooring, Chinese men in Portuguese-style sailor suits jump ashore at the last minute and the *King Yan* slowly steams out of the Baia de Praia Grande and into the South China Sea. Leaning on the rail, watching the lights of Macao behind them, she hears the man exhale for the first time.

*

On the deck of the *King Yan* she sits close enough to the Englishman to appear familiar. He smokes constantly. They buy some fruit from an old Chinese lady to eat. They take a late dinner in the *King Yan*'s small dining room. They do not talk. They only nod to the captain when he passes by them. The Englishman's Spanish is only marginally better than hers, that is to say, minimal to non-existent. He admits it is the most basic schoolboy Spanish at best. They do not wish to be overheard speaking English. She speaks precious little French; he no German whatsoever. And so he remains silent, and she respects that.

The Fort Bayard Wharf, 1931

The crossing to French territory is sixty miles or so, skirting the eastern coast of Hainan Island, and they reach Fort Bayard the following evening shortly after nightfall in a tropical downpour. In the moonlight they see the French tricolour flying over the barracks building of the Fourth Regiment of the Tonkinese Rifles.

This time Chinese men in French-style sailor suits with pompoms on their hats appear on the arc-lit jetty to grab the ropes and tie up the *King Yan*. The gangplank is lowered and the passengers begin to disembark.

There is a moment of nervousness as they approach the immigration shed and see a French official waiting. Another tricolour, hanging limply, dripping wet in the downpour. A signboard reads…

FORT BAYARD
TERRITOIRE DE LA RÉPUBLIQUE DE FRANCE

First there is a rush of Chinese peasants with heavy canvas bags, goods to be traded from Macao to Fort Bayard. Then old women with small children. A few more Chinese – these better dressed, in western suits. Finally, a few Europeans – French residents of Fort Bayard, she assumes – saunter forward, assured of their citizenship here. The couple form the rear of the disembarking passengers. Each holds a suitcase in their outer hands while their inner hands are lightly touching – outwardly a couple, bracing slightly against the falling rain, tired after their voyage.

The French official appears half asleep, his blue *kepi* pulled low, a Tilley lamp swarmed by mosquitoes in the glow. He is obviously tired, homesick and a little hung-over. Lounging nearby, paying no attention to the arriving passengers, are two Annamese soldiers of the Tonkinese Rifles in their distinctive uniform.

The ruse works: her Spanish passport and his forged immigration permit pass muster with the French customs officer. They are moving on, leaving French territory for Sumatra, ceasing to be his or France's problem. He does no more than merely glance at them, and at their vaccination and inoculation certificates, offers a Gallic shrug, half-heartedly stamps their papers and touches his fingertips to his *kepi* to usher them on. The world is in turmoil, but this agent of France's *Extrême-Orient* colonial empire seems not to care for anything but returning to his sleep, escaping the humid night and the swarms of mosquitoes that buzz around his lamp. These two are the last passengers from the *King Yan* and his work is done.

*

A French Consul resides at Fort Bayard with little more to supervise than some surrounding farmland, a few hopeful Catholic missionaries, and some small trade between Kwangchowan and French Indo-China. But, crucially, Fort Bayard is not Japanese-occupied; it has declared for Vichy, an ally of Tokyo, and so it has been left alone. They know that there is little here beyond a Posts and Telegraphs  office, an *École Franco-Chinoise*, a hotel, some Western-style buildings, mouldering godowns and a regimental barracks. The only building of any grandeur noted in the encyclopaedia she consulted in the Biblioteca Pública was reputedly the Hôtel du Résident Supérieur, the territory's Government House.

They walk to Fort Bayard's only hotel, the Grand Hôtel des Fort Bayard, which, as far as they can tell, is

The Fort Bayard Hotel, 1930s

deserted and lacking in guests. They rent a room and sit on the bed, waiting. She takes the chance to wash and freshen up. The hotel interior is an almost exact copy of any French provincial establishment.

From Macao, John Reeves had warned agents of Free China to expect them. Before they can think of sleep, the French manager of the hotel knocks on their door to tell them that there are some Chinese gentlemen waiting for them in reception. Clearly this route has been used before. The manager, who could be running an almost identical hotel in any French town, is seemingly unfazed by three unshaven and dirty Chinese men armed with rifles in his lobby and lounging on his verandah to keep out of the rain.

The partisans lead the way out of Fort Bayard, into the fields of Kwangchowan beyond and then, by daybreak, along the banks of Rivière Ma-The, out of Vichy French territory and into the dawn of Free China.

The next few weeks are spent moving across country, village by village, passed from guide to guide, travelling largely at night, sleeping by day in farm buildings or on stone floors, reliant for food on Free China villages, ever onwards inland towards Chungking, China's wartime capital 900 miles north. From Chungking there is the possibility of a British or American plane to Rangoon, maybe as far as Calcutta… so the rumours in Macao had said.

We can follow her this far, but alas no further. The available and surviving records show that he made it – that he contacted the British Embassy in China's wartime capital. But of her? Of this orphaned German-Jewish girl with a Spanish passport and an entry visa to Great Britain, Her Protectorates and Territories, obtained in Macao from John Reeves, we know nothing more.

We must assume she got to Chungking as there is no mention of trouble on the way. He lives on in the records – an Englishman; a man of some importance to the war; a man with a continuing role to play. But she, a Jewish refugee still a long, long way from somewhere permanently safe, slips from history… We can only hope she made it somewhere safe eventually.

*

In the cafés surrounding the Largo do Senado, in the cheap *pensão* of the Rua do Campo and the Rua da Barca da Lenha; in the billiards room and the back yard of the Aurora Portuguesa hotel, in the makeshift synagogue of the Biblioteca Pública, in the government refugee camps of Dr. Lobo, the rumours persist:

> *Royal Navy submarines have been spotted at sea. They will surface at night and take refugees to British India;*

> *The United States Air Force flies offshore at night and has planes that can land on water to take people away;*

> *The Swiss Red Cross are arranging an evacuation ship to take us all to New Zealand and a new life;*

> *There are jobs in Sumatra, in the oil fields. You must work for the Japanese, but they will feed you;*

There is a French port, not far away, in China, controlled by General de Gaulle's men, where you can get a boat to England;

There was one girl here, from Shanghai, and they say she got to Free China, that she is safe now.

Others, though, remained...

Reuben, Lefko, Ruckenstein, Kohn, Rosenblum...
Cohen, Weinbaum, Montefiore, Schlagman, Pollack ...
Fabritsky, Chaimowitz, Spielmann, Kahn, Herzberg...
Berger, Levy, Silberstein, Sachs, Weiss...

They sit and sip the last of their ersatz coffee dregs late into the hot night; sleep eludes them in the humidity; they just toss and turn uncomfortably. They write more letters to relatives who may have made it to Shanghai. No replies ever come. They count out their last patacas, thinking they can maybe afford another bowl of noodles, another cup of coffee. They feed on rumours... they survive on gossip... ever more rumour and gossip... the eternal pastime of the refugee. But still there is some hope left... in Macao.

THE END

Emigranten Thrift Shop – a charitable clothing store for Jewish refugees initially funded by Sir Victor Sassoon and housed in one of his properties at 55 Nanking Road (now Nanjing East Road)

Annamese – a term common at the time to describe Vietnamese people

Tonkinese Rifles – otherwise the *tirailleurs tonkinois*, a corps of Tonkinese (north Vietnamese) light infantrymen led by French officers. The French used them widely in China and French Indo-China

Rivière Ma-The – the Maxie River or, in Chinese, the Maxie He

Macao and World War II
A Timeline

March 1932 – Following Japan's invasion and annexation of Manchuria (subsequently renamed Manchukuo), Portugal's foreign minister, Fernando Augusto Branco, issues a statement of neutrality in the Sino-Japanese conflict at the League of Nations headquarters in Geneva.

August 1937 – Chinese activists and intellectuals in Macao establish the Salvation Society of Macao (SSM) to raise money for the Chinese war effort against Japan and also to help refugees arriving in the Portuguese colony.

May 1938 – Portugal stations troops on the neighbouring islands of Lapa, Dom João and Montanha (now Wanzai, Small Hengqin and Great Hengqin), just to the west of Macao. Lisbon hopes that these will eventually become a formal part of Macao's territory. In 1941 Japan ordered Macao to surrender the islands and they were occupied by Japanese troops. In 1945 they were returned to Nationalist China and they are now part of the Zhuhai Special Economic Zone.

October 1938 – Following the Japanese invasion of China and the occupation of Canton (Guangzhou), Macau starts to become a refugee centre, causing the Portuguese-controlled enclave's population to swell from approximately 158,000 people to 245,000 in 1939, and then to more than 450,000 within a few years.

March 1940 – Japanese troops continue to invade southern China and are stationed approximately twenty miles from the Macao border. However, they advance no closer and respect Portuguese neutrality. There is a significant influx of Chinese refugees from Guangdong province into Macao.

October 1940 – Navy commander Gabriel Maurício Teixeira assumes the post of Portuguese Governor and Commander-in-Chief of Macao, with Major Carlos da Silva Carvalho as his chief of staff.

June 1941 – John Pownall Reeves arrives in Macao to become British Consul.

December 1941 – Hong Kong falls to Japanese forces on Christmas Day. As a Portuguese colony, Macao is left as a neutral enclave now entirely surrounded by Japanese-held territory. Nine thousand British subjects become refugees from occupied Hong Kong in Macao along with all Macanese returning from Hong Kong and any Portuguese who had been living there. Macao's population is further swelled by refugee arrivals to approximately 500,000 people.

February 1942 – Japanese troops invade both Portuguese and Dutch Timor to oust the small and under-equipped combined British, Australian and Dutch force occupying the territories. This sparks fears that Japan will occupy Macao next. However, the Japanese opt once again to respect Portuguese neutrality in Macao.

November 1942 – In Shanghai the idea of a restricted Ghetto for Shanghai's stateless Jewish refugees is approved by the Japanese authorities.

December 1942 – Conditions in Macao hit a new low point due to combined wartime privations, food shortages, multiple disease outbreaks in the refugee camps, and a particularly cold winter, resulting in a record 16,000 deaths (the average had been three to four thousand per annum throughout the 1930s).

February 1943 – In Shanghai the Japanese authorities declare a "Designated Area for Stateless Refugees" and order those Jews who arrived in the International Settlement after 1937 to move within it.

May 1943 – In Shanghai the Hongkew Ghetto, the "Heime" or "Little Vienna", begins formal operation – barely three quarters of a square mile and home to 17,000 Jewish refugees, as well as the roughly 100,000 Chinese already living there.

August 1943 – Japanese troops seize the British-owned steamer *Sai On* in Macao. Macao police attempt to resist the seizure, and twenty are killed by Japanese soldiers.

September 1943 – Japan demands the installation of Japanese "advisers" to oversee Macao. If their request is refused, Tokyo argues, the only alternative is full military occupation. Consequently a virtual Japanese protectorate is created in Macao.

February 1944 – In an effort to crack down on rampant smuggling and the spread of the black market, Governor

Gabriel Maurício Teixeira bans the use of Chinese money and insists only specie issued by Portugal's overseas Banco Nacional Ultramarino will be legal tender.

January 1945 – The United States claims that "neutral" Macau is planning to sell aviation fuel to Japan. Aircraft from the carrier *USS Enterprise* bomb and strafe the hangar of the Macao Naval Aviation Centre, targeting the fuel dump, as well as killing five civilians and destroying a maritime museum.

February & June 1945 – American Air Force raids follow in February and June on strategic targets including the Porto Exterior and the Dona Maria II Fort. Following the Japanese surrender, the Portuguese government protest and, in 1950, the United States pays US$20,255,952 compensation to Lisbon.

August 1945 – Japan surrenders unconditionally and Macao returns to unfettered Portuguese control.

September 1945 – On September 3rd the Shanghai Jewish Ghetto is officially liberated.

Escape from Macao

There were indeed a number of recorded escapes from Macao to southern China during the war. Most went via the route used in this story – by boat to the French-controlled territories of Fort Bayard and Kwangchowan, and then onwards, via a long trek, into Free China. The escapes went on throughout the war and many did involve the connivance and support of the British Consul in Macao, John Reeves. A number of escapees from Hong Kong's Stanley Internment Camp did manage to get to Macao and then, some with and others without Reeves's help, managed to escape to Kwangchowan and on into Free China.

Perhaps the best known of these escapes, which was undertaken with the blessing of Reeves, is that described by Phyllis Harrop in her autobiography *Hong Kong Incident*. British, and having arrived in Macao after escaping from Hong Kong, six weeks after its fall on Christmas Day 1941, Harrop managed to join a sizeable group of French refugees from Hong Kong who boarded a ferry to Kwangchowan that sailed via Macao. They arrived at Fort Bayard at about 10am in the morning. Harrop's steamer was captained by a man called Bertillot, 'an old China coast skipper', known to one of her party of French escapees from Macao. Port officers and the French police boarded the vessel but Harrop was allowed to go ashore. She then managed to get from Kwangchowan across unoccupied China to the wartime capital of Chungking.

Another notable escape occurred in April 1943. An American, Lowell B. Davis, contracted with Macanese smugglers (who are also described in the British archives as 'guerrilla leaders') to take a party of Americans and Filipinos to the southern Chinese coast. John Reeves asked Davis to take a number of British subjects seeking to escape Macao with him. Davis agreed. Eventually the Davis party totalled 37. Due to rapid inflation Davis was also told that, in terms of paying both the smugglers and various conduits along the way in China, goods were now preferable to money and so the escape party also had a large amount of luggage, much of which was lost en route.

Despite fewer boats than originally agreed with the smugglers, and the constant threat of patrolling Japanese naval craft, the party did manage to reach an unoccupied strip of coast not far from Hong Kong. From there they eventually managed to rendezvous with American forces in Guilin, in Free China, that June. The United States Air Force was then able to transport the party out of China to British-controlled India.

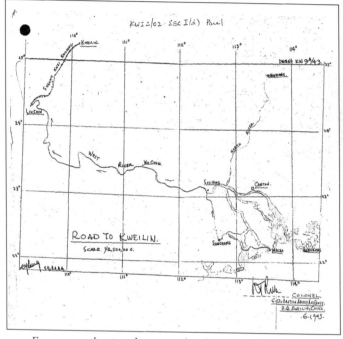

Escape map showing the route taken by the Lowell B. Davis party, 1943

Further Reading

On Macao:

Austin Coates, *Macao and the British: Prelude to Hong Kong, 1637-1842* (Oxford University Press, 1966)

Maurice Dekobra, *Macao, Enfer du Jeu* (in French) (Editions Baudinière, 1938)

Geoffrey C. Gunn, *Wartime Macau: Under the Japanese Shadow* (Hong Kong University Press, 2016)

Hao Zhidong, *Macau: History and Society,* (University of Washington Press, 2011)

Phyllis Harrop, *Hong Kong Incident* (Eyre & Spottiswoode, 1944)

Christina Mui Cheng, *Macau: A Cultural Janus* (Hong Kong University Press, 1999)

C. A. Montalto de Jesus, *Historic Macao* (Kelly & Walsh Shanghai, 1902)

Donald Pittis & Susan J. Henders, *Macao: Mysterious Decay and Romance* (Oxford University Press, 1997)

Philippe Pons, *Macao* (Reaktion Books, 2002)

Jonathan Porter, *Macau: The Imaginary City* (Westview Press, 1999)

John Pownall Reeves, *The Lone Flag: Memoir of a British Consul in Macao During World War II* (Hong Kong University Press, 2014)

José Rodrigues Dos Santos, *A Amante do Governador* (a wartime Macao-set novel in Portuguese) (Gradiva, 2018)

On Kwangchowan:

Alfred Cunningham, *The French in Tonkin and South China* (Hong Kong Daily Press, 1902)

François Boucher, *The Jungle of Surprise* (CreateSpace, 2015)

Robert Nield, *China's Foreign Places: The Foreign Presence in China in the Treaty Port Era, 1840-1943* (Hong Kong University Press, 2015)

See also the excellent short documentary on Kwangchowan, *The Ghost Colony*, by François Boucher (available on YouTube)

On Jewish Shanghai in World War II:

Ursula Bacon, *Shanghai Diary: A Young Girl's Journey from Hitler's Hate to War-Torn China* (M Press, 2004)

I. Betty Grebenschikoff, *Once My Name was Sarah: A Memoir* (Original Seven Publishing, 1993)

Ernest Heppner, *Shanghai Refuge: Memoir of the World War II Jewish Ghetto* (University of Nebraska Press, 1993)

Kathy Kacer, *Shanghai Escape* (Second Story Press, 2013)

Vivian Jeanette Kaplan, *Ten Green Bottles: The True Story of One Family's Journey from War-Torn Austria to the Ghettos of Shanghai* (St. Martin's Press, 2004)

Rena Krasno, *Strangers Always: A Jewish Family in Wartime China* (Pacific View Press, 1992)

Rena Krasno & Audrey Friedman Marcus, *Survival in Shanghai: The Journals of Fred Marcus, 1939-1949* (Pacific View Press, 2008)

Sam Moshinsky, *Goodbye Shanghai: A Memoir* (Real Film & Publishing, 2016)

Ester Benjamin Shifren, *Hiding in a Cave of Trunks: A Prominent Jewish Family's Century in Shanghai & Internment in a WWII POW Camp* (CreateSpace, 2012)

Sichmund Tobias, *Strange Haven: A Jewish Childhood in Wartime Shanghai* (University of Illinois Press, 2009)

Acknowledgements

An earlier version of this text first appeared in *Cha: An Asian Literary Journal*, Issue 33, September 2016. My thanks to the founding co-editor Tammy Ho Lai-Ming.

A slightly longer version of this text was then recorded for RTHK Radio 3 in Hong Kong as a four-part series abridged and narrated by myself. Many thanks to Phil Whelan at RTHK for commissioning and recording that. It is available on the RTHK podcasts site, via their app or at http://podcast.rthk.hk/.

My thanks to Gary Brown and Stef of Vibe Books in Mui Wo, Lantau Island, Hong Kong for hosting me for a week when we were recording.

Colin Day and Elizabeth Ride kindly shared their research with me concerning wartime escapes from Macao to Free China. Elizabeth graciously allowed me to reproduce the escape map too. The map is from KWIZ (Kweilin Weekly Intelligence Summary) No. 2, dated June 15, 1943.

Documents relating to the Lowell B. Davis escape party are part of the Research Centre Collection of the Australian War Memorial in Campbell, Canberra – AWM PR82/068 Series March 10, 1941. AWM is where much of the archive of the British Army Aid Group (BAAG) that operated in wartime Macao and Southern China is housed.

Anne Witchard kindly edited and commented on the evolving manuscript over several incarnations. Catherine Tai designed the cover. And thanks to Pete Spurrier and Blacksmith Books for publishing this version of *Strangers on the Praia*.